Peter Roop and Connie Roop

TAKE COMMAND, CAPTAIN FARRAGUT!

illustrated by Michael McCurdy

Atheneum Books for Young Readers
New York London Toronto Sydney Singapore

For La, who enthusiasticaly shares America's stories with her students.
For Jake, who has taken command of Harba's Watch!
—P. R. and C. R.

To Bren Murcia, who is already a lover of books.
—M. M.

Atheneum Books for Young Readers
An imprint of Simon & Schuster Children's Publishing Division
1230 Avenue of the Americas
New York, New York 10020

Book design by Edward Miller
The text of this book is set in Packard.
The illustrations are rendered in scratchboard.

Printed in the United States of America
First Edition
10 9 8 7 6 5 4 3 2 1

Library of Congress Cataloging-in-Publication Data
Roop, Peter.
Take command, Captain Farragut! / by Peter and Connie Roop.—1st ed.
p.   cm.
Includes bibliographical references.
ISBN 0-689-83022-X
1. Farragut, David Glasgow, 1801-1870—Juvenile literature. 2. Admirals—United States—Biography—Juvenile literature.
3. United States. Navy—Biography—Juvenile literature. 4. United States—History, Naval—to 1900—Juvenile literature.
[1. Farragut, David Glasgow, 1801—1870—Childhood and youth. 2. Admirals. 3. Diaries.]
I. Roop, Connie. II. Title.
E467.1.F23   R59 2001
973.7'5'092—dc21
[B]   00-038612

The cruise of the Essex

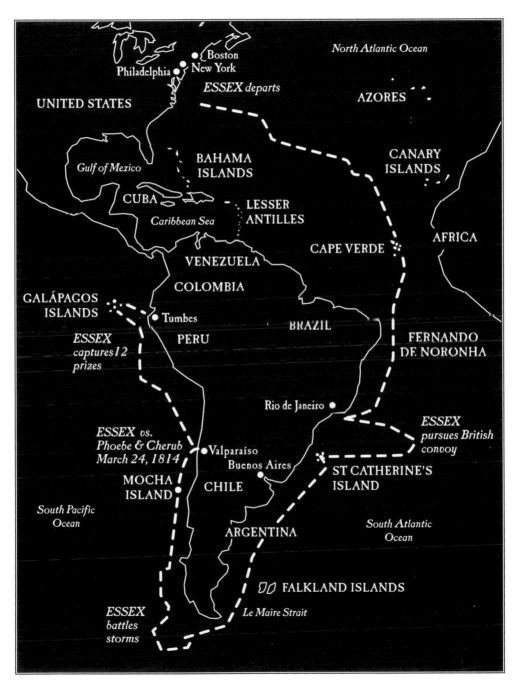

Prison Ship
Valparaíso, Chile

Tuesday, March 29, 1814—Day One of Our Captivity

Dear Papa,

    I begin this letter not knowing if it will reach you. I often think of you, especially now, as I have much time on my hands. I am a prisoner of the English in Valparaíso. I was captured after a fierce battle on Valparaíso Bay.

    I think, too, of Mama and miss her. For the year we were together Mrs. Porter loved me like her own son, but it was not the same. And then I went to sea.

    I hope you read this letter with patience and understanding. I know I have been wayward in not writing you for more than two years, but you'll see much has happened to me in that time. In this letter I hope you will see that the boy you sent to be cared for by Captain Porter has grown into a man.

    Now as a man I must suffer this imprisonment. We hope to be paroled soon. If so, we will be exchanged for British officers and returned to the United States. I do not look forward to the parole. Parole means I may not fight the English again until I am exchanged for a British midshipman. If we are not paroled, however, we will be shipped to England. There we will rot in another dreadful prison ship.

As with my other challenges, I must face this one with courage and determination.

I shall write daily to you long letters, just as a midshipman I wrote daily in my log. I will tell you my adventures to the best of my memory, beginning with my posting to the *Essex.*

The *Essex,* having been shattered by cannon fire, is now in the hands of the English. Yet the day I first walked her decks, her black paint was fresh, her tall masts stood firm, her white sails were furled, her crew was eager to engage the English enemy.

I was the last new midshipman to climb the *Essex*'s rope ladder.

I will continue in my next entry, for I am tired after this harrowing day.

Good night, Papa.

∘ ∘ ∘ ∘

Wednesday, March 30, 1814—Day Two of Our Captivity

I still remember the day I left you in Louisiana to join Captain Porter's family. Mama's death was so sudden. So painful to endure. But now I understand better why I had to leave you. Perhaps then I could not understand that, alone, you could not care for me and all my brothers and sisters.

Like a flapping sail, I was pulled in two directions. I envied brother William in his glorious midshipman's uniform. I so wished to follow in his footsteps. Yet I longed to remain with you. Not to be torn from my family. Little did I understand the challenges I would face when I left that sunny day with Captain and Mrs. Porter. Every day since, I have taken a moment to bring a picture of you and Mama to my mind. Now as you read this letter, I hope you will see me in your mind. I have done much and experienced many things following the wind and the waves aboard the valiant *Essex.* When Captain Porter was ordered to Washington, I followed.

I first set foot on the *Essex* on August 9, 1811. Commander Bainbridge had posted Captain Porter to the *Essex.* Much to my delight Captain Porter desired I should serve him and our country as one of the *Essex's* midshipmen. Anchored in Newport News, Virginia, we awaited Captain Porter's orders to sail. The *Essex,* carrying forty-six cannons, was prepared for war against England. We called this our Second War of Independence. Just as you fought in the first war, I was to fight in the second.

I berthed with the eleven other midshipmen. At ten years of age, I was the youngest. And the smallest. Like you, Papa, I fear I will never grow outwardly big, but must grow large within myself.

John Fittermary is the eldest midshipman. His spirits always seem bright. Even now, imprisoned as we are, he finds something for us to laugh at. The other middies tease him, calling him Mary, which brings color to his face. I have learned much from him, including how to better hold my temper in check. Fittermary calls me a firecracker, always ready to explode. Such a fiery temper must come from our ancestors, Papa, for in this way, as in my size, I am much like you.

Captain Porter says I am the youngest midshipman ever to serve in the United States Navy. This also means I am the youngest midshipman ever captured. I remember the pride I felt when, nine months earlier, Captain Porter read my midshipman's warrant out loud. I have read it so many times myself that it remains in my memory to this day, as does the oath of allegiance I swore to the navy.

JAMES MADISON, PRESIDENT OF THE UNITED STATES OF AMERICA. To all who shall see these presents, GREETINGS; KNOW YE, That reposing special Trust and Confidence in the Patriotism, Valor, Fidelity, and abilities of David Farragut, I do appoint him a Midshipman in the NAVY OF THE UNITED STATES. He is therefore carefully and diligently to discharge the duties of a Midshipman. And I do strictly charge and require all Officers, Seamen, and others under his command to be obedient to his orders as Midshipman. Given under my Hand, at the city of Washington this seventeenth day of December in the year of our Lord one Thousand eight hundred and ten, and in the thirty-fourth year of the Independence of the United States.

JAMES MADISON

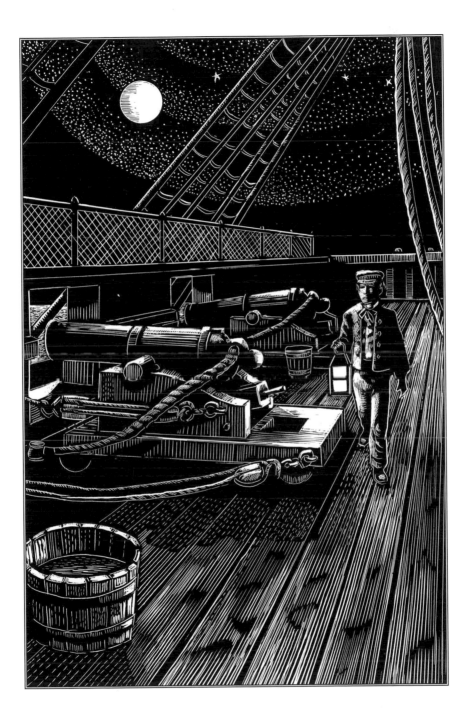

Now the sun sets. Across the water I hear English bells ringing a change in the watch.

How well I remember my first watch. Midnight until four in the morning. I found it difficult to stay awake, though the stars dazzled me. To fight sleep I walked from bow to stern and back again, treading those decks I would come to know so well. Here I tread the same number of steps, imagining the *Essex* beneath my feet.

At the end of my watch I slept for four hours, until eight bells, then the day began anew. I dozed during my lessons that day, earning a sting from Lieutenant Downes's "starter," the rope he snapped to urge along slackards. Never again was I to feel its bite!

If I were aboard the *Essex*, I would be hanging my hammock now, which is not such an easy thing to do. That first night I battled my hammock, spilling myself onto the gun deck. I fought two other middies when they laughed at me. Fittermary showed me how to balance properly so I would stay in the hammock. I was pleased, for I feared I would have to fight every midshipman that night before I could sleep.

The hard deck of a prison ship is my bed these nights.

Good night, Papa.

◦ ◦ ◦ ◦

Thursday, March 31, 1814—Day Three of Our Captivity

Another dawn. I write early today to spare our few candles so we can tend the wounded in this damp gloom. The English supply us with ink, quills, and paper, for they treat us like gentlemen and officers, but they will give us no more candles.

Captain Porter ordered me to tally our losses from the recent battle against the *Phoebe* and the *Cherub*. Two English ships against our one. We lost fifty-eight men to cannon fire and thirty-one to drowning. Sixty-six men lie wounded. The *Phoebe* is as damaged as the *Essex*. My temper flares. The English flag flies from the *Essex's* mainmast. How I long once again to see the Stars and Stripes flutter there as it did when I first joined the *Essex*.

My early days aboard the *Essex* passed in a maze of activities.

"Mr. Farragut, report to deck. Mr. Farragut, do your sums. Mr. Farragut, fetch the carpenter. Mr. Farragut, calculate our position. Mr. Farragut, Mr. Farragut, Mr. Farragut…" In my dreams I heard calls for Mr. Farragut. Yet I was pleased to hear the *Mr.* before my name, as it meant I truly was an *Essex* officer.

Now I long for those duties. In captivity boredom is our greatest enemy, not the English. As I sharpen my quill this morning I am reminded of my first knife, the midshipman's dirk Captain Porter presented to me.

How I envied him his long, strong sword. A dirk is a puny weapon, yet it was all we middies were allowed to carry. Swords we had to earn through skill, courage, and luck, all of which would lead to promotion. I vowed to someday have a sword as grand as Captain Porter's.

Yet today his sword and mine are in the hands of the English, tokens of our surrender.

Yes, Papa, even though it is months before my thirteenth birthday, I have earned and worn my own captain's sword.

My greatest fear those early days on the *Essex* was that I could not meet the challenges before me. Captain Porter would not, and still will not, tolerate anything less than perfection in each man under his command. Those not meeting his standards were dismissed. I hoped never to suffer such disgrace. I met the daily schooling with pleasure, as each new lesson I mastered moved me closer to earning my sword. The mathematics drill, the endless navigation calculations, the tedious grammar, all I faced with determination. I gained on the older midshipmen, for such learning comes easy to me. I helped other middies with their studies, earning friends as well as knowledge.

Yet, try as I might, I could not make friends with Will Odenheimer. He was my tormentor, finding ways to upset me, or spoil a completed task, or make me look foolish in front of the men. He was sixteen years old and much larger than me, so fighting him was out of the question. More than once I used my wits to turn his schemes astray, but then he would simply find another way to torment me. Then one time I truly bested him.

As the youngest midshipman, I had to obey the orders of

anyone my senior. Will challenged me to climb to the lookout's post atop the mainmast.

He did not know I love to climb. I remembered the towering pine by our home on Lake Pontchartrain. I scampered up that tree like a monkey. From the deck the mainmast seemed no taller than my pine.

I was proved wrong. Climbing a tree anchored in earth is ever so much different from climbing one anchored in water.

With my companions watching, I climbed to the boom with no difficulty. I looked up. I seemed no closer to the crow's nest.

Then I made a mistake. I looked down. The mast swayed as the *Essex* rocked. I almost lost my grip.

But the ring of challenging faces far below spurred me on. A wave of dizziness washed over me. I closed my eyes.

Hand over hand I climbed. Up and up and up until I thought I must soon touch a cloud. Not once did I look down until I reached the top.

Newport News lay before me like a miniature town. Churches were dollhouses. People, horses, cows, and pigs, like toys.

Lieutenant Downes's fierce command brought me sharply to my senses. "Mr. Farragut, report to the deck. Immediately!"

Back on deck Lieutenant Downes appeared angry. He was in charge of the midshipmen at the time. His word was law to us.

"Mr. Farragut, why did you climb the mainmast?" he asked.

"I wished to see if Captain Porter had a fire burning in his lodgings, sir," I replied.

His gaze traveled over the faces of the other midshipmen. Behind his stern glance he seemed to be smiling at me. Turning on his heel, he went below deck.

Will Odenheimer, who would have lost his midshipman's privileges if I had reported him to Lieutenant Downes for ordering me to do such a dangerous task, grasped my hand in newfound friendship.

I had met his challenge. Since then we have been as close as brother William and I used to be.

Papa, I never knew I could write so much! Tomorrow I will tell of giving my first order.

○ ○ ○ ○

Friday, April 1, 1814—Day Four of Our Captivity

There is no tomfoolery today. Even Fittermary is quiet as we await word of our fate. Captain Hillyar of the *Phoebe* will tell Captain Porter at noon what is to become of us. We must obey Hillyar's orders, be they parole or prison.

Thinking of orders reminds me to tell you, Papa, of giving my first order to a sailor. I had worried much about giving someone a command, for I was so young and the sailors so old.

It came about this way. Lieutenant Downes needed Boatswain's Mate Kingsbury. I asked Kingsbury to report to deck. He looked as if he'd squash me like a weevil from a biscuit.

"I am not obeying any pip-squeak," he bellowed at me.

I was frightened—he was so large and old, old enough to be my grandfather.

I asked him again. Once more he refused.

I then ordered him, saying, "Kingsbury, report to deck. Immediately!" in my best imitation of Lieutenant Downes.

With a grumble, Kingsbury obeyed.

I feared I had made an enemy of Kingsbury. Now that Will was my companion, would another foe take his place? *Why can't we just fight the English, not ourselves?* I wondered. If I could not order a man to deck without a struggle, how would I ever become a captain? Was I really too young to be a midshipman, as I had overheard some claim?

The following day Kingsbury again challenged me. I ordered him forward to help the boatswain. Cupping his ear, he pretended not to hear me. I sternly commanded him. Shuffling his feet, he slowly obeyed.

I was frowning outside but grinning inside, Papa. This time Kingsbury had followed my order after only the second request. I hoped my next order would need to be issued but once.

Captain Porter is to report to Captain Hillyar within the hour. Will we ever see the distant shores of America again? Or will we be taken captive of England to rot to death on prison ships? Papa, I shiver as I remember the tales you told of your captivity on a prison ship during the Revolution.

o o o o

Saturday, April 2, 1814—Day Five of Our Captivity

Our greatest fear has passed. We will not be sent to England! The *Essex Junior* will take us to the United States where we will be exchanged for an equal number of English prisoners. The officers had their swords returned. I polished mine until it gleamed like a dolphin slicing through the sea.

Now that our last battle has been fought, I will tell the story of my first fight. And it was against our own countrymen!

This battle happened before we left American shores. We remained anchored at Newport News. Barrels of food, casks of fresh water, rope, tar, sails, and hundreds of other supplies were brought daily to the ship. Each day Captain Porter attended the ship's business ashore.

Knowing my skills in a small boat, for he had sailed with us many times in Louisiana, Captain Porter placed me in command of his gig. Each morning a small crew of men and I were to take the captain to shore and return him to the *Essex* when his business was concluded.

That fateful morning we rowed to the dock to wait for the captain. I was afraid, for my enemy, Kingsbury, was steering. I feared he would not obey my orders.

We tied to the dock to await the captain's return. A crowd of townsfolk gathered idly to watch us.

My face burned red when one said, "Here's a pint-sized captain dressed in his prettiest uniform. He even has a toy sword

to protect us from the English." I tried to ignore him. Soon his companions taunted me.

Kingsbury suggested that we go to another dock.

"No," I said in a voice loud enough for the townsfolk to hear. "These idlers are on navy property. If they are looking to fight the United States Navy, we will give them a battle!"

One idler picked up a bucket of dirty water. He poured it on me! Before I knew what had happened, Kingsbury snagged the culprit with a boat hook and spilled him into the gig. No matter his dislike for me, Kingsbury was not going to allow an *Essex* officer to be ridiculed.

Having recovered, I leaped from the boat, yelling, "At them, men!"

Armed with oak oars, we battled the unruly townspeople, who hurled rocks at us in return. We fought them off the dock and into the town square, where a shrill whistle ended the battle. The town police corralled us and led us to the courthouse. As the officer in charge, I signed a peace warrant, pledging us to keep the peace or go to jail.

Captain Porter must have known of the fight, but he said not a word until we returned to the ship. There he explained our adventure to Lieutenant Downes, saying "I could use more midshipmen like Mr. Farragut. That lad is three pounds of uniform and seventy pounds of fight!"

Kingsbury, his left eye black, grinned at me. I had met another challenge.

o o o o

Wednesday, April 6, 1814—Day Nine of Our Captivity

Papa, I have not written for several days, as the wound in my arm pains me so. Please do not worry. It is but a scratch received in the battle with the *Phoebe*. Dr. Hoffman assured me the wound was properly cleaned; it will heal with only a scar to remind me of the fight.

We learned today we will set sail on the tide on April 27 aboard the *Essex Junior*. She will be stripped of all her weapons and rendered defenseless. I anxiously await that date as I did the day the *Essex* set sail in 1811, for I wish to be free once again to twist the English lion's tail!

It was late August of 1811 when Newport News finally disappeared behind us and the Atlantic spread before us. My eyes hurt from the strain of looking for English ships. We saw none. Fittermary told me we would not see many. Captain Porter was sailing south, far from the prying eyes of the British, where he would forge us into a fighting crew. Still, I looked for sails whenever I was off duty.

As midshipmen we had no regular duties to perform as the sailors did. Instead we had four hours of classes, followed by four hours of study, in which we mastered the art of navigation, learned to read charts, did math, and learned grammar and a host of other subjects. It was like school on land except for the roll of the ship and the constant sounds of the ship's timbers creaking, the men talking, orders being shouted, sails flapping, and the waves dashing against our sides. The *Essex* seemed to me like an eagle searching for her prey. Alas, now she is an English ship, an enemy ship.

One evening Captain Porter read us our orders from Commodore Rogers. Although we were not yet at war, we were to stop all English ships. If any resisted, we would engage them in battle. With the crew I cheered until my throat grew sore.

Captain Porter ordered me to raise our new flag. In tall blue letters it read, FREE TRADE AND SAILORS' RIGHTS. Thus we declared to the English to leave our sailors and ships alone or suffer the consequences.

Alas, that proud flag is now in English hands, too. What humiliation.

I hurrah for the Stars and Stripes!

∘ ∘ ∘ ∘

Thursday, April 7, 1814 — Day Ten of Our Captivity

When we were captured, I had nothing left to me but the pocket watch Captain Porter had given me the Christmas I became a midshipman. Inscribed on its cover is this treasured message: D. P. TO D.G.F., U.S.N., 1810. I hid it from the thieving hands of the English sailors.

Looking at the watch now reminds me of timing my gun crew during gunnery practice.

As we sailed south, Captain Porter pushed us hard. We drilled without stop until the men could load the guns and run them out in less than thirty seconds. I timed the men on my guns until we proved we were among the fastest crews aboard.

For target practice we floated empty barrels a half mile away. The gun crews took turns trying to hit them. My crew missed so many times, I despaired for them. Yet they did not give up. When they finally hit a barrel, they cheered mightily. With practice our accuracy improved.

Captain Porter ordered us to use powder and ball. Fittermary told me no other ship practiced with powder and ball. Captain Porter did this so when we actually engaged a ship under fire, our men would know how best to judge the distance and accuracy of their shots. Fittermary said Captain Porter was determined to make the *Essex* the best American ship afloat. And Papa, he did, earning a commendation from Commodore Rogers.

Such practice held us in good stead, as you shall see. That is, until our misfortune with the *Phoebe*. She will be a long time being repaired, however. Captain Porter said we placed eighteen twelve-pound shots into her hull, three below the waterline. My crew hit her twice, I know. If only we had placed more balls into her, the English would be the prisoners, not us! We did fire seventy-five broadsides at her!

I was slow to learn to live with only four hours of sleep at a time. I did enjoy the midnight watch, especially when the stars sparkled. Fittermary said if we ever sailed south of the equator, we would see different stars. I found this hard to believe until I saw the Southern Cross myself. It is grand beyond words. I can glimpse it from our porthole, a shining reminder of the freedom that will soon be ours.

○ ○ ○ ○

Friday, April 8, 1814—Day Eleven of Our Captivity

As we are to be paroled, Captain Hillyar accepted Captain Porter's word that none of us would try to escape. Thus we have been granted freedom from our damp prison and released to live in tents on the beach.

The surgeons are much pleased, as the fresh air has already worked wonders with the men's spirits and health.

We built great fires, as winter is approaching. I think of spring in America, but here on the opposite end of the earth the seasons are opposite, too. The flickering flames bring to mind the many fire drills Captain Porter made us practice. As you know, fire is a sailor's most feared enemy.

Whenever "Fire! Fire!" was shouted, it was as if an anthill had been kicked open. The men grabbed their weapons and fire buckets and scurried to their posts. My post was at the stern, ready to lower our flag in case we must abandon ship. I hoped never to perform that sad duty!

Yet it was for me to obey Captain Porter's orders to strike our colors before the *Phoebe* sank us. I had never disobeyed any

order before, and I was tempted to ignore this one. The screams of the wounded men, mingled with the cries of those struggling in the water, forced my hand to the halyard to reluctantly lower the Stars and Stripes. Much to his discredit, Captain Hillyar fired upon us for a full ten minutes longer before stopping. In that time four men near me died. And this after our colors were struck!

My hatred for the English knows no bounds.

Yet, Papa, the many fire drills rewarded us once in a most timely fashion.

That tale I will tell when next I pick up my quill.

∘ ∘ ∘ ∘

Saturday, April 9, 1814—Day Twelve of Our Captivity

As you know, war was finally declared against England on June 18, 1812. Supplied and ready for battle, we sailed on July 3 (two days before my eleventh birthday) to meet the enemy. Our months of preparation would finally be put to use. Independence Day was celebrated with cannon salutes at dawn, noon, and sunset. We searched for the enemy with determination.

I hope you read about our exploits that summer. Within a month we had captured nine English merchant ships with no damage to ourselves! The men were excited, for we were to share prize money.

But no warship had fallen into our hands. We were eager to test ourselves against an English fighting ship.

Then, on August 13 we faced our greatest foe to date, HMS *Alert*. Captain Porter lured the *Alert* close to us. We dragged a canvas sea anchor to disguise our real speed while flying the hated Union Jack.

Falling for our trick, the *Alert*, her guns rolled out, closed with us. On Captain Porter's signal we opened our gun ports and raised the Stars and Stripes. We fired a broadside, came about, fired another. The shot from my gun crew shredded her mainsail.

The *Alert*, overpowered, struck her colors. By my watch, the battle lasted eight minutes from first shot to last!

Earlier we had sent a number of the *Essex*'s men to bring our nine prize merchant ships to shore. Most of the *Alert*'s crew were brought aboard the *Essex* as prisoners. Consequently they greatly outnumbered our depleted crew.

The third night after the *Alert*'s capture, I had fallen asleep when a strange noise awakened me. Opening one eye, I peered into the gloom. One of the *Alert*'s officers, armed with a pistol, was staring at me! I pretended to sleep, waiting until he passed.

Then I slipped silently to Captain Porter's cabin, woke him, and told him of the prisoner's escape.

He leaped from his bed, flung open his cabin door, and shouted, "Fire! Fire!" The men of the *Essex* silently flew to their stations. The men from the *Alert* shouted in confusion, making themselves known to us, and thus were easily captured again.

Captain Porter reported my actions in his log, the first time I have received such praise. I fell asleep hoping it would not be the last. I dreamed that night of someday boarding a ship, my own captain's sword flashing.

○ ○ ○ ○

Sunday, April 10, 1814—Day Thirteen of Our Captivity

Papa, I had saved a newspaper article telling of our exploits but fear it was lost with my other things in the near destruction of the *Essex.* I had planned to mail it to you before we began this long voyage, but being involved in so many things, I neglected to send it. As you are a sailor yourself, I know you will understand the many things that must be done aboard ship.

We did not know it in the fall of 1812, but we had secret orders to sail to the Pacific to capture English ships there. Never before had an American warship sailed these waters. We would be the first, along with the other two ships of our squadron, the *Constitution* and the *Hornet.*

However, we failed to meet them at our rendezvous. It being November, Captain Porter determined to sail into the Pacific alone. On the way I had a most curious adventure.

Spirits ran high on the *Essex* as we sailed south. Every day was warmer than the one before. We shed the chill of New England for the warmth of the tropics.

I awoke on November 23 eager for the day ahead, for Fittermary had told me we would cross the equator that morning. I reached for my log to record this event but could not find it

anywhere. At breakfast I saw Fittermary slipping weevils into my porridge as he went to his watch on deck. I knew he enjoyed jokes, but this was going too far. I made up my mind to confront him. As I reached the deck I was grabbed from behind. I twisted until I saw that it was George Hill, an ordinary seaman, pinning my arms. All around me the other middies squirmed like eels in the arms of their captors.

We were dragged across the deck to a crowd of sailors dressed as women in an odd collection of rags, ripped sails, and old clothes.

On a barrel, his face painted green, sat William Kingsbury, ruling the riot as King Neptune.

"From this day forth, these poor creatures shall be my servants. Anoint them," he roared.

Sailors ran forward with a bucket of an evil-smelling mixture of soap and tar. One by one we were taken to the bucket and had our faces covered with the concoction.

I struggled to break free.

"Mr. Farragut does not want to be my servant," snarled Neptune. "Let him be shaved last!"

I watched as each new servant was made to sit on a rail over a barrel of water while his face was shaved with pieces of wood. When the shave was finished, he was shoved into the barrel. Then he joined in the fun of watching the rest of us endure this torture.

The sticky mess had dried to my face before my turn came.

The wood razor burned as it dragged across my skin. The water cooled my burning face, and the extra food and drink for all my hands eased my anger.

Several sailors brought out their violins. We danced into the afternoon, thus celebrating the crossing of the equator.

Now that I am a true "servant of Neptune," I will never have to undergo such torment again. Yet all who first cross the equator must partake of this ritual of the sea. It was but a minor challenge, but a major discomfort! I smile, imagining Captain Porter suffering such humiliation his first time.

Good night again, Papa.

o o o o

Monday, April 11, 1814—Day Fourteen of Our Captivity

The ground where we have our tents on Valparaíso Bay seems so solid after months aboard the *Essex*. Yet rounding Cape Horn on our way to the Pacific, many were those who prayed to set foot ashore again, even for a brief moment. I was among them.

Papa, my words cannot adequately tell of the terror and hardships our rounding of the Horn entailed. The frequent storms were first friendly, blowing us westward, forward. Suddenly the wind became our enemy, battling us, pushing eastward back along our route. We fought to stay away from the barren, ice-shrouded shore, knowing if forced against the rocks, we would all perish. Following the storms would come days of drifting calm. Then once again the ocean would try to turn us back, sending towering waves against us, tossing the *Essex* as a wild horse tosses its mane.

We ran short of food. Gone were the fresh fruits, pigs, chickens, and turkeys we had gotten in Brazil. The peas and beans had been spoiled by saltwater seeping belowdecks. The kegs of meat became so rotten we dumped them overboard to the pack of hungry sharks trailing us.

One night I awoke, dreaming of roasting meat. But the smell was so real I slipped from my hammock to find the source. One of the men was cooking Jimmy, his pet monkey, while others stood watching, licking their lips in anticipation. Despite my hunger, I returned to my hammock. *As an officer, should I have stopped them?* I wondered.

The men grumbled constantly, debating whether we should proceed or turn tail. Never once did Captain Porter waver in his determination, not even when we almost foundered and sank.

It happened this way.

I was standing the third watch when another storm crashed upon us. Mountainous waves rose before us in an instant. Captain Porter came on deck just as a wave broke over the bow. The deck disappeared as the wave crashed back toward the stern. I was swept off my feet. I grabbed a rope and hung on. Suddenly my left arm felt as if it had been hit by a cannonball. A spar, broken by the wave, had smashed into me. I let go of the rope and would have been swept overboard had not a strong hand gripped me.

It was Captain Porter.

He thrust me against the wheel. Blinking saltwater from my eyes, I saw five other men struggling beside the captain to steer the ship. Together we had to keep her bow into the wind, or the waves would break over us broadside and send us deep to Davy Jones's locker.

A hatchway cover had been washed away. Above the roar of the wind I heard someone shout, "We're sinking!"

My heart stopped, *My arm is broken,* I thought. *I can't even swim now.* Yet I still did my part, struggling with the wheel. Kingsbury bellowed in his bull-like voice, "We are not sinking, you lubbers. Get to your feet and get the pumps going! Another wave like that will send us to the bottom if you don't get pumping!"

The storm held us in its terrible grip for five days. When at last it blew itself out, fewer than a dozen men had escaped injury. Almost everyone had at least a smashed toe or finger. My arm was severely bruised, not broken. Captain Porter suffered so many bruises that the doctor ordered him to bed.

The deck looked as if it had been blasted by cannon fire. The men went to work with a fever, and within two days we were ship-shape again. Limping, but shipshape.

Lieutenant Downes read Captain Porter's list promoting fifteen men for their actions during the storm.

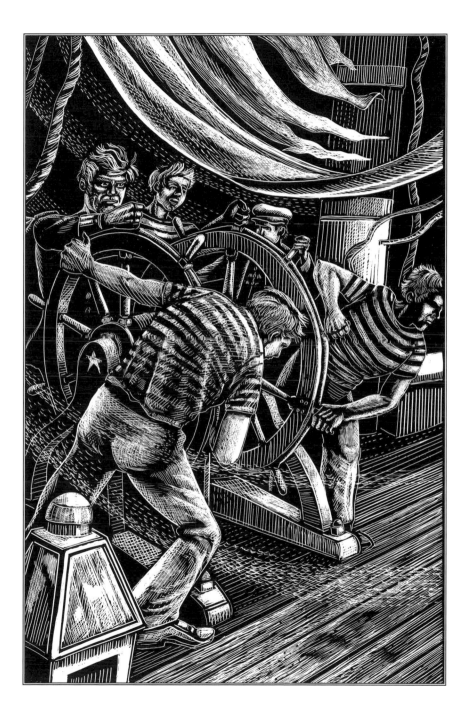

Papa, I must admit, I cried myself to sleep that night, for my name was not among them.

What more must I do, I wondered, *to prove my mettle?*

My time would come, dear father, but not fast enough for me.

∘ ∘ ∘ ∘

Tuesday, April 12, 1814—Day Fifteen of Our Captivity

I am up with the sun this morning. As I gaze around Valparaíso Bay, I am reminded of when we first reached these shores.

Finally we had rounded the dreadful Cape Horn and turned north into the Pacific. Despite the hardships, our spirits rose once again, knowing we had accomplished something no other United States warship had ever done! Now we must find English ships to capture. Before that, however, we had to refit at Valparaíso.

Our greeting from the Chileans was warm and wonderful. They had no love of the English themselves. I joined Captain Porter and the other officers on a round of gala parties and dances in our honor.

When the *Essex* was resupplied and seaworthy, we sailed again in search of English ships. Unaware of our presence, the English were not prepared. We easily captured two vessels, the *Georgiana* and the *Policy.*

After their capture Captain Porter congratulated us (I was

with Lieutenant Downes when we boarded the *Georgiana*). He said "Fortune has at length smiled upon us, because we deserved her smiles. The first time she enabled us to display FREE TRADE AND SAILORS' RIGHTS in these waters, she put in our possession near a half million dollars' worth of the enemy's property. We will yet render the name *Essex* as terrible to the enemy as that of any other vessel!"

And we did. We captured vessel after vessel.

Most of the ships we captured did not fight us, for they were whaling ships. At first disappointed (for I wished to battle each ship), I came to realize the value of what we were doing. Many of the ships were sent to Valparaíso to be sold as prizes. The money thus gained aided our war effort. The supplies we took off each ship kept us in good stead.

Three of the ships we renamed and they became our companions. Lieutenant Downes, second in command to Captain Porter, captained the *Essex Junior*. Where once we had been only one ship, now we were a squadron.

Each time a ship was taken, Captain Porter assigned the highest ranking officer to her as acting captain. Each night before I slept I counted the officers ahead of me—ten midshipmen plus higher officers. Even as quickly as we captured ships, it would be months before all eighteen were taken and I was made a captain.

Papa, my captain's sword came much sooner than I expected or had even dreamed of.

Before I relate that, however, I must tell you the story of the Battle of the Galápagos Islands.

∘ ∘ ∘ ∘

Thursday, April 14, 1814—Day Sixteen of Our Captivity

This morning, heavy rains fall and the wind whips across the bay. The rain had dampened our spirits somewhat, but I laugh out loud when I think of the fearsome Battle of the Galápagos (as the men now call it).

We had sailed to the strange and wonderful Galápagos Islands. These islands are frequented by whaling ships, but no people live on the bare volcanic rocks. Instead, lizards crawl like ancient dragons along the shores. Finches unlike any I have ever seen flock here, as do dozens of other birds. Black crabs, camouflaged against the rocks, scurry in and out of the water. Volcanoes light up the sky at night like vast bonfires. But the most curious and delightful creatures are the lumbering tortoises that dot the land like sea-tossed boulders.

These tortoises are so great that I could ride them. I climbed upon a broad back, grasped the shell, and slowly trundled along aboard a four-hundred-pound behemoth!

We caught many of the beasts for food, their meat the sweetest I have ever eaten. Their fat was relished as better than butter!

The morning of the infamous battle I was guiding the gig to

shore with Captain Porter aboard when we saw a beach packed with sea lions. These monsters, despite massive, blubbery bodies, seemed harmless enough. The captain suggested we kill one to see how it tasted.

Armed with oars and boat hooks, the men leaped onto the beach and ran after one large sea lion as it waddled away. They hit it over the head, but it kept heading toward the safety of the water.

Kingsbury, never cowed in a fight, grabbed the beast by its tail. The lion roared, and flipped Kingsbury head over heels into the surf as it made good its escape.

I laughed so hard my sides felt as if stabbed by my dirk.

Undaunted the men pursued an even bigger creature. The sea lion growled, shaking its bulk with anger. Then it turned its furious eyes toward me!

I, too, made good my escape, leaping into the gig. With unimaginable speed the monster pursued me, scattering the captain and the crew in its wake. Snorting like a bull, it brushed the gig aside as if it were driftwood, and the sea lion disappeared underwater.

Thus it was that Captain Porter lost his first and only battle of the entire voyage—that is, until the treachery of Captain Hillyar and the *Phoebe.* But before I write about that sad final chapter of our voyage, I will at last tell of my captain's command. As I have exhausted my supply of ink, I must wait until I can obtain more from the English. Thank goodness I am an officer and treated as such. My only remaining possession is my watch, and only death will pluck it from my hand.

o o o o

Friday, April 15, 1814—Day Eighteen of Our Captivity

Two days have passed since I last had both ink and time to write. The *Essex Junior* has been stripped of her guns. We are preparing her for the voyage back home. I have resumed my midshipman's duties during the day as we make her shipshape. Thus I can spare only a few minutes to continue my story. My wish is to finish this lengthy letter before we sail. I hope to post it here with a Chilean vessel sailing before us to New Orleans with a load of hides. This way it will reach you sooner than if I carry it myself. My fears are that, as an unarmed American vessel, we might still fall prey to an English ship and have our papers destroyed.

Captain Porter is doing likewise through a Chilean friend here. He has promised to include my letter with his official papers. It is his hope that they will reach the United States quickly, so that the government is alerted to our misfortune.

My captain's sword hangs from the tent post, the sun reflecting off its scabbard. It is hard to believe that a year ago I wore it as a captain of the *Barclay!*

Tomorrow I will tell that tale, as I am called to duty now.

o o o o

Saturday, April 16, 1814—Day Nineteen of Our Captivity

We had sailed from the Galápagos in search of English ships. We captured several and sent them as prizes to Valparaíso. Still, many more would have to fall to our guns before I would be placed in command. I said nothing to Captain Porter of my desires. He must have known. One day he called me before him as we chased another English whaler.

He handed me his spyglass and said, "Take a good look at her, Mr. Farragut. She will be *your* first true command."

My hands shook so, I could not hold the glass steady. "She sails well," I managed to say.

"She's heavy," Captain Porter said. "Her holds are full of whale oil. She'll earn us a pretty penny in prize money."

I gave him back the spyglass and he said, "David, I have watched you these months, especially facing the dangers rounding the Horn. Ordinarily I would have named John Cowan as the next prize master. However, Lieutenant Downes recommended *you* above all of the other midshipmen for a command if we captured another vessel. You have earned the respect of all the men and officers aboard the *Essex.*"

I saluted Captain Porter, unable to say anything for fear I would trip over my tongue.

"Every captain has his own sword, Acting Captain Farragut." Then he handed me a sword and belt much like his.

Without another word he ordered a warning shot fired at the enemy ship. I watched the ball splash ahead of the vessel. Knowing it was a lost battle, she dropped her sails and lowered her flag in surrender.

"Captain Farragut, pick six men to take as your boarding crew. Report to me in ten minutes."

My feet felt as anchors. I couldn't budge.

"Take command, Captain Farragut. Immediately!"

I shook the cobwebs from my brain. I was a captain at last!

"Aye, aye, sir," I said, and dashed to select my men.

I picked Kingsbury and five others who had fought by my side on the streets of Newport News.

Even before we reached the decks of the *Barclay*, I smelled the stench of the whale oil. I brushed its unpleasantness aside, thrilled to be assuming command of a ship.

As we approached the *Barclay* her men peered over the railings. A red-bearded fellow glared fiercely, his gaze not unlike that of the sea lion. I assumed he was captain and was soon proved correct.

Now, Papa, I will describe the following events to the best of my recollection. I was so excited that many details disappeared from my mind.

I climbed the rope ladder first and waited for my men to join me.

The red-bearded fellow stepped forward, towering above me like a mast. "I am Captain Randall," he boomed. "And who might you be, runt?"

"I am Captain Farragut. You, sir, are my prisoner."

He roared with laughter. "What has happened to the American navy that they make mere boys prize matters?"

"For your knowledge," I informed him, "we have captured so many English vessels that our powder monkeys will be given commands soon."

He snorted.

"Now, sir," I said. "Order our men to raise the main-topsail. We are to fall in with the *Essex Junior*."

"I'll shoot any man who touches a rope," bellowed Captain Randall. "As for you, Farragut, you'll find yourself off the coast of New Zealand in the morning. I'll go my own course. I will not trust myself with a damned nutshell!" He spun way and disappeared down a hatch.

I froze, Papa, not certain what course to take. I looked around for help, then realized I was indeed in command and must take charge. Our other ships were already underway. I had to act quickly so we would not lose them.

"If he so much as shows his head above deck," I commanded, "throw him overboard! Now raise that main-topsail, and be quick about it."

"Aye, aye, Captain Farragut," said Kingsbury, a huge grin on his face.

Gripping his pistol, he stood by the hatch. When Captain Randall reached the deck again, he stared into the muzzle of Kingsbury's pistol.

The *Barclay* was soon underway, and we fell in behind the *Essex Junior*, leading the other prizes toward Valparaíso.

Papa, I must stop. My weary arm feels as if I had practiced sword fighting for hours.

◦ ◦ ◦ ◦

Sunday, April 17, 1814—Day Twenty of Our Captivity

I hardly slept that night, Papa, for fear that Randall would try to retake his ship. How well I remembered the escaped prisoners aboard the *Essex!* I need not have feared, however, for Randall realized the hopelessness of his situation, especially with the *Essex Junior* within hailing distance should he attempt to retake his ship. He stayed below and out of my way until we reached Valparaíso Bay.

Those brief days as captain of the *Barclay* were among the happiest of my life. The men of the *Barclay* were a well-trained lot (I must give Captain Randall credit for that). We had no unfortunate incidents to mar our voyage. The *Barclay* was not fast, laden as she was with whale oil. Three weeks passed before we saw the peaks of Chile rising on the horizon. I did not mind our slowness, for each day pleased me so as ship's captain. Having been in command yourself, Papa, you know the joy and responsibilities that come with a captain's sword. Even if I never sail again (which is an impossible thought!), I will treasure my time commanding the *Barclay*. And I not yet thirteen at the time.

Tomorrow I will conclude this letter. Once again I apologize, dear Papa, for being so tardy in writing you. My moments aboard the *Barclay* were much like riding a cresting wave only to find the wave carrying me onto a rocky shore. That rocky shore was the capture of the *Essex*.

◦ ◦ ◦ ◦

Wednesday, April 20, 1814—Day Twenty-three of Our Captivity

Dear Papa, I must quickly conclude this letter. It must be aboard the *Santiago* within the hour, as she sails on the tide this afternoon.

I must therefore save telling you of my further adventures and leap ahead to our battle with the *Phoebe* and the *Cherub.*

Last fall we learned the English had sent several warships to capture us. We entered Valparaíso Bay on February 3, to resupply quickly and set to sea again. Unfortunately, the *Phoebe* and the *Cherub* came upon us, blockading the entrance to the harbor and preventing our escape.

For the next six weeks we played cat and mouse with the enemy vessels, the *Essex* trying to slip to freedom, the *Phoebe's* fifty-six guns blocking us. On March 28, Captain Porter saw our opportunity. The wind was from the east. The English ships stood far out to sea. We signaled the *Essex Junior* to fall in behind us and set sail.

No sooner had we rounded the point than the fickle wind changed. It turned from the west, aiding the English and preventing our escape. A sudden squall hit us, carrying off our main-topmast and the two men atop it. Crippled, we tacked and reentered the harbor. We anchored a pistol shot from shore in neutral waters. The English, unwilling before to follow us into port, trailed us and opened fire.

For more than two hours we exchanged broadsides, giving as well as we got. But the *Phoebe* carried more cannons than we. Her firepower, combined with that of the *Cherub*, severely damaged us.

Carrying a message to the gun deck, I was wounded. A cannonball smashed into the ship, showering the deck with flying splinters. One splinter, as sharp as an arrow, pierced my arm.

With fewer than seventy-five of our crew still standing, Captain Porter ordered me to lower our flag. For the first time I almost disobeyed an order. Nevertheless, I forced my hand to grasp the halyard and lower the Stars and Stripes.

Harder yet was relinquishing my captain's sword after our surrender. I now know why Captain Porter, gallant to the end, surrendered, for he could no longer shed our blood in the face of such overwhelming odds. My pain was nothing to what seared his soul that fate-filled day.

Papa, the *Santiago* has just fired her stern chaser, signaling her departure.

I close now, praying this letter reaches your hands. I eagerly await the day when I can tell you the rest of my adventures in person.

Until then, I remain,
Your obedient son,
David Glasgow Farragut,
Captain, United States Navy

Glossary of Nautical Terms

bells: strokes on the ship's bell, used to tell time at sea. The day is divided into six watches of four hours each; one bell marks the end of the first half hour, and eight bells the end of each watch. Twelve A.M. or P.M. is always marked by eight bells.

boat hook: a pole with a point and a hook for moving objects, including boats, into place

boatswain: the officer in charge of sails, rigging, anchors, and cables on a ship

boom: a long, round piece of wood lashed to and used to extend the lower edge of a sail. Often referred to as a spar.

bow: the front end of a boat or ship

crow's nest: see *lookout's post*

deck: a platform that serves as a floor on a ship or a boat

frigate: a high-speed, medium-sized, three-masted vessel used in war from the seventeenth to the nineteenth century. More maneuverable than larger ships, frigates carried twenty-four to thirty-eight guns on a single gun deck and were used mainly as lookouts or escorts for convoys.

gig: a long, narrow, light ship's boat used to travel between ships or from ship to shore

gun port: a square hole cut in the side of a warship, through which a cannon was fired

hatch: an opening in a ship's deck, used for passage of persons or cargo from one deck to another

hatchway: the vertical space between a series of hatches, one below the other, linking the upper and lower decks of a ship

hold: a large compartment in the lower part of a ship, used mainly for storage of cargo, gear, and provisions

lookout's post: a small, partially enclosed platform high up on the mast of a ship

mainsail: the principal and usually largest sail of a sailing vessel

mast: a tall pole, or spar, that supports the sails and rigging of a ship. Square-rigged vessels such as frigates had three masts: the mizzenmast at the stern, the mainmast in the center, and the foremast in the bow. Each mast usually supported five or six sails.

midshipman: an officer in training, equal to today's rank of naval cadet

port: a harbor with facilities for docking ships and taking passengers and cargo

powder monkey: a small boy whose job was to carry gunpowder to the cannons

prize: in naval terminology, something taken by force or threat, such as a ship and its cargo, lawfully captured at sea in time of war

prize crew: the officer and sailors in charge of taking a naval ship into port after it has been captured by a boarding crew

rigging: all ropes and chains used on a

ship to support and control the sails and spars

square rig: an arrangement of sails and masts in which the principal sails are basically rectangular and are fastened to poles (called yards) that, at their center, are fastened at right angles to the masts

stern: the rear end of a boat or ship

stern chaser: a cannon at the back (stern) of a ship

tack: to turn a sailing ship to a different course

topsail: the second sail up from the deck

warrant: a certificate of appointment for an officer who ranks below a commissioned officer

watch: the period of time (usually four hours) a crew member is on duty; also the sailor or group of sailors on duty at a particular time

Bibliography

Farragut, David Glasgow. Correspondence and documents. United States Naval Academy, Nimitz Library, Annapolis, MD.

Farragut, Loyall. Ed. *David Glasgow Farragut, First Admiral of the United States Navy (embodying his Journal and Letters)*. New York: D. Appleton and Co., 1879.

Gerson, Noel B. *Clear for Action!* New York: Doubleday, 1970.

Gruppe, Henry E. *The Frigates*. Alexandria, VA: Time-Life Books, 1979.

Harding, Richard. *USS Constitution: Old Ironsides*. Little Compton, RI: Fort Church Publishers, 1991.

Mahan, Alfred T. *Admiral Farragut*. St. Claire Shores, MI: Scholarly Press, 1970.

Mercer, Charles. "The Youngest Captain." *Boys' Life*, May 1986, 17–21.

Porter, David. *Journal of a Cruise*. Annapolis, M.D.: Naval Institute Press, 1986.

Authors' Note

Glasgow Farragut, born July 5, 1801, began his naval career at age nine, the second youngest midshipman ever commissioned in the United States Navy. When he was twelve, Glasgow had his first command: acting captain of the *Barclay*, a captured British ship. When he died in 1870, Farragut was a Civil War hero as well and admiral of the United States Navy, the first person ever to hold that rank.

As a boy Glasgow loved sailing ships. His father frequently took him on sailing expeditions on Lake Pontchartrain, Louisiana, near their home. Glasgow set sail whenever he could, the wind, water, and wooden boat his only companions.

When Glasgow's mother died in 1809, his father placed him in the care of his friend, Commodore David Porter. When Porter was posted to Washington, D.C., Glasgow accompanied him, never to return to his Louisiana home. Glasgow held Porter in such admiration that he changed his first name from Glasgow to David in his honor. Under the commodore's guidance, David applied himself to his schoolwork, yet his heart was set on joining the navy. In 1810, David's wish came true—President James Madison signed his midshipman's warrant. Tension between the United States and Great Britain was building. War seemed likely. David joined Porter aboard the frigate *Essex*, cruising the American coast, hunting for British ships to capture. In 1812, when war broke out, the *Essex* became the first American ship to defeat a British warship.

David Glasgow Farragut spent his life aboard ships or helping to direct naval operations. When the Civil War erupted, southern-born Farragut remained with the United States Navy, choosing not to break the oath he had taken as a boy. Farragut led the capture of New Orleans, opened the Mississippi River for Union gunboats, and won the Battle of Mobile Bay (the last Confederate stronghold on the Gulf of Mexico)—three critical victories for the Union. At Mobile, Farragut said those famous words: "Damn the torpedoes! Full speed ahead!"

Using Farragut's own accounts of his life as a midshipman, as well as Captain Porter's journal of the cruise of the *Essex*, we have told the story of David's early days in the navy, days when the courage of the boy demonstrated the heroism of the man he was to become.

Research for this book was undertaken at the United States Naval Academy in Annapolis, Maryland, and aboard the frigates *Constellation* and *Constitution*. The authors would like to thank Mr. James Cheevers, curator of the United States Naval Academy Museum, for his help on details of Farragut's life, and Mary Rose Catalfamo, special collections librarian at the United States Naval Academy's Nimitz Library, for her assistance in locating Farragut's original letters. Readers wishing to see the actual watch Farragut was given by David Porter will find it on display at the United States Naval Academy Museum. Those wishing to walk the decks of a frigate should visit the USS *Constitution,* anchored near Boston, Massachusetts. Nicknamed "Old Ironsides" because cannonballs bounced off her oak sides, the USS *Constitution* is the oldest warship still on duty in the United States Navy.